Danny Bear Joins the Teddy Ten... Academy

Contents
		Page

Chapter One
A flying start!

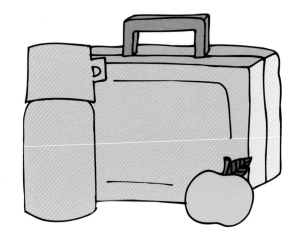

Danny Bear woke up early.

The sun was shining through his window, the birds were singing and the bees were busy buzzing.

Danny, a tubby, friendly bear with thick, soft brown fur and chubby paws, got out of bed, stretched and yawned a little.

"This is definitely a something-to-do day," he said to himself, as he bounced down the stairs to the kitchen.

His brother Johnny Mac and sister Chloë had left the remains of their breakfast on the table: crusts of buttered toast and honey; an empty boiled eggshell; and a large, half empty jug of apple juice. "Humpff," said Danny, "they're already out playing Teddy Tennis."

As Danny wandered around the kitchen humming his favourite tune, he came across Chloë's packed lunch box sitting by the cooker. "Not like my sister to forget her lunch box. I'll take it over to her at the Teddy Tennis Academy, after I've had a little breakfast for myself."

So after breakfast Danny left his home in Honeycomb Lane with Chloë's packed lunch under his arm.

As he got close to the Academy he heard a strange noise - pop - pop - pop…
"What is that?" Danny thought, as he looked through the fence to see what was going on.

He saw a big, strong bear with a smiling face and large ears chasing a red and yellow tennis ball. Written on the back of his t-shirt were the letters C H A R L I E. "That must be his name," thought Danny. Charlie took a mighty swing at the ball and it flew back over the net. Much to Danny's surprise, on the other side of the court, was his big brother, Johnny Mac. Johnny Mac moved towards the ball, took a smooth swing and it glided back over the net. Charlie saw the ball coming, ran for it and dived with his racket. He hit the ball, 'Pow!' but it flew over the net and right out of the court, landing at Danny's feet!

"Game to me!" shouted Johnny Mac. Then he saw his little brother watching.
"Surprise, surprise! What brings you here Danny?" said Johnny Mac smiling.

"Chloë forgot her packed lunch so I thought I'd bring it to her," Danny explained.

"Come and meet my friend Charlie and then we can go and find Chloë together,"
said Johnny Mac.

Danny walked through the gates of the Teddy Tennis Academy feeling very excited. He looked up at the big strong bear smiling down at him. "Good to know you, young Danny," Charlie Bear said. "How does it feel to be the brother of the best Cub Cadet in the Teddy Tennis Academy?"

Danny looked up. "Well, um…er…haven't given it much thought," he said shyly.

Charlie Bear looked surprised. "Johnny Mac, is Danny joking?"

"No," said Johnny Mac, "I haven't really told Danny anything about Teddy Tennis. I wanted him to find out for himself."

"What is there to find out?" asked Danny.

Charlie looked down at Danny and started to chuckle, then he began to laugh. Then Johnny Mac grinned and he began to laugh. "What's going on," thought Danny. Soon, the whole Academy had come to a complete halt. Cub Cadets of all stages were rolling around laughing. Then Danny looked up and saw a big grown up bear walking towards them.

"Here comes Head Ted, the teacher in charge of all Teddy Tennis," said Johnny Mac.

"What's going on, Johnny Mac?" said Head Ted.

"Well, my little brother, Danny, wonders what there is to know about Teddy Tennis," said Johnny Mac.

"Let's give Danny a Teddy Tennis racket, and he can find out for himself," said Head Ted smiling. "Amanda Panda, please let Danny use your racket for a moment!"

"Okay," said Amanda Panda, the smallest of the Cub Cadets, handing over her racket.

"Now, young Danny," said Head Ted, "I'm going to hit the ball over the net and you're going to hit it back to me. We have to keep the ball going over the net until one of us makes a mistake."

Danny listened and thought for a while. "How do you make a mistake?" he asked.

"Good question," said Head Ted. "If you hit the ball out of the court area, or if you hit the ball into the net, or if you let it bounce twice, or you miss the ball completely, they are all mistakes, which means I win a point."

"Oh, that sounds simple enough," said Danny.

"Let's have a go then," said Head Ted.

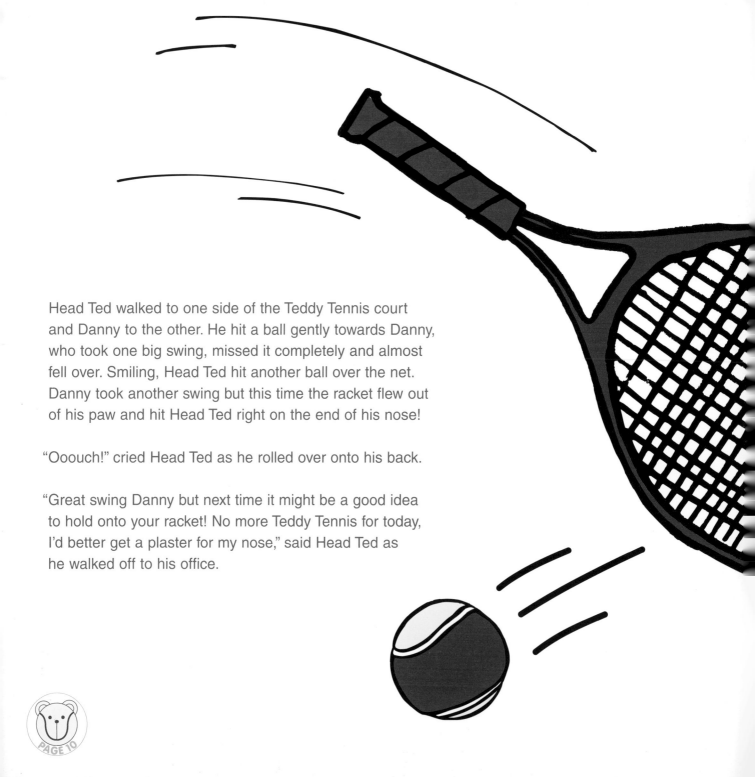

Head Ted walked to one side of the Teddy Tennis court and Danny to the other. He hit a ball gently towards Danny, who took one big swing, missed it completely and almost fell over. Smiling, Head Ted hit another ball over the net. Danny took another swing but this time the racket flew out of his paw and hit Head Ted right on the end of his nose!

"Ooouch!" cried Head Ted as he rolled over onto his back.

"Great swing Danny but next time it might be a good idea to hold onto your racket! No more Teddy Tennis for today, I'd better get a plaster for my nose," said Head Ted as he walked off to his office.

Chapter Two
Happy Honey Pots

That night, Danny couldn't sleep. First he lay on his left side, then after a while he lay on his right. A minute later he changed his mind and lay on his left side again. This went on for quite a while, but he simply could not get the picture out of his mind, of Amanda Panda's racket flying through the air and hitting Head Ted slap bang on the end of his nose. How silly! What would all his friends think of him now! "Sleep, sleep, I must sleep," he said to himself. Then he remembered what Grandma Bear always told him:

"Lie on your back and count pots of honey, and you'll sleep till dawn and wake up sunny."

When Danny woke up the next morning he knew he wanted to be a Teddy Tennis champion. So after breakfast he went straight down to the Academy.

When he arrived he saw Johnny Mac and Charlie talking with Head Ted.

Danny took a very deep breath and said to himself,
"These few small steps for me are one big step in the right direction."
Then he strode up to Head Ted.

"Sorry to disturb you, Head Ted, d'you know what?!!"

HONEY

Head Ted, who now had two plasters criss-crossed on the end of his nose, looked round and down at Danny. "What, young Danny?" he said with a smile.

"I've given it a lot of thought and I've decided I want to join the Teddy Tennis Academy and become a champion like my big brother Johnny Mac," explained Danny proudly.

"You have, have you?" said Head Ted. "Well, come and stand by the height-o-meter to see if you are tall enough to become a Teddy Tennis Cub Cadet."

Danny followed Head Ted to his office, and there, beside the door, was a thin black line and above it, in large red capital letters, were the words:

"ABOVE EIGHTY CENTIMETRES - JUST RIGHT"

…and below the line were the words:

"BELOW EIGHTY CENTIMETRES - TOO SMALL FOR THE MOMENT"

Danny looked at the line, stood up as straight as he could, took a deep breath and stepped forward.

"I'm afraid, you're five centimetres too short. Eighty centimetres is Cub Cadet entrance height and you're spot on seventy-five. The reason is simple," continued Head Ted, looking down at Danny who was trying not to appear too upset. "Cubs under eighty centimetres are not ready for Academy training. Each Cadet must be ready to learn to hop, skip, jump, run, and be able to throw a ball and catch a bouncing ball. And last but not least, all Cub Cadets must be able to tie their own shoe laces in under one minute, without Mama or Papa Bear's help."

"Oh," said Danny, looking down at his trainers which Mama Bear had neatly tied that morning.

Danny wondered if he should tell Head Ted that it soon would be his fourth birthday and that he was expecting to be doing a lot of growing at any moment, but he thought better of it and said nothing.

"I'll be back," said Danny and waved good-bye to Head Ted. He didn't give up; he knew there had to be a answer to his problem. The problem was finding the solution.

"A glass of apple and blackcurrant juice and a few moments to think should do the trick," he thought. After a long time and a lot of thinking, the problem was still there. Just as he was deciding that bed was probably the best place to be, Chloë came clumping down the stairs.

"I'm off to Amanda Panda's birthday party," she said.

Danny looked at his sister. Her big eyes were gleaming under the light of the kitchen lamp. "Something is different," said Danny.

"Apple blossom conditioner and rose petal scent," said Chloë looking pleased.

"No, no, nothing to do with smells. Something has changed," said Danny looking at his sister's clothes more closely. He studied each piece of clothing, starting with the top and finishing with the trousers.

"Yes," said Chloë, "new top, new trousers and my trendy, new, pink, platform trainers!"

"Those trousers are baggier and have more pockets than Uncle Christopher's gardening dungarees! I can't even see your trainers!" Danny exclaimed, peering down to where Chloë's feet ought to be. "Here they are," said Chloë, lifting the folds of pink cotton from the floor. Danny looked down at the pink and white trainers and slowly went down on all paws.

Suddenly, Danny jumped up and started bouncing around the kitchen like a baby kangaroo. "Happy-honey-pots! I have found the solution to my problem! I have found the five centimetres I need!" he shouted.

"Mama! Papa! Danny has gone bananas," yelped Chloë.

A moment later Mama and Papa Bear came rushing down the stairs to the kitchen. "What's all this noise about?" asked Mama Bear, looking at Danny who was still bouncing around.

"I found the solution to my problem!" shouted Danny.

"What solution? What problem?" asked Papa Bear.

"It's like this," explained Danny, "I want to join the Teddy Tennis Academy and need to be eighty centimetres tall. I'm seventy-five centimetres, but if I wear platform trainers, my new height will be eighty centimetres. Problem solved!"

Chapter Three
Bear in Training

Danny thought that one day was not really long enough for Head Ted to believe he had grown five centimetres, so he decided to leave it for two weeks. He also felt he needed to practise all those things Head Ted had told him he should be ready to learn as a cub cadet.

Much to the amazement of the whole family, at seven fifteen each morning, Danny would spring out from his bedroom in his favourite red tracksuit bottoms and his new sky blue t-shirt with the words, 'Bear in Training' written in bold on the front and practise his running, hopping and skipping. He then did some kind of bear 'Tai Chi,' which Amanda Panda had told him about.

"Breathe in slowly through the nose and out through the mouth, bend the knees, paws out as if holding a large green balloon and think of nothing," said Amanda Panda.

"That last bit's easy," thought Danny.

Every day Danny practised throwing and catching a ball. He counted how many catches he could do and how many times he could throw the ball at a target. Danny found that his catching and throwing were getting better and better. He was so pleased with himself. He even practised tying his shoe laces and he got better at that too!

Finally came the day when Danny felt the time was right to go and see Head Ted. He had bought the same platform trainers as Chloë, but in white, and some 'wicked' baggy tracksuit bottoms.

He arrived at 11.30, just as Head Ted was finishing a lesson with the stage three Cub Cadets.

"What can I do for you, Danny?" he said, smiling.

"I have been doing a lot of growing lately. This is because of my new healthy diet of fruit and vegetables, my fitness training and the sunny weather we have been having," said Danny, trying not to look at his feet.

"I see," said Head Ted looking closely at Danny. "You do seem a bit different. Well, follow me to the Cub Cadet height-o-meter."

Once again Danny stood beside the office door. This time the top of his head was well above the thin black line, where it read:

"ABOVE 80 CENTIMETRES - JUST RIGHT"

ABOVE EIGHTY CENTIMETRES
- JUST RIGHT

"How very strange" said Head Ted looking at Danny, "you seem to have grown at least 10 centimetres!" Danny was so surprised he fell over his own feet!

Danny looked up at Head Ted, Head Ted looked down at Danny.

"You certainly can't play Teddy Tennis in those trainers," said Head Ted laughing. "You can't even walk in them. You need good Teddy Tennis trainers if you want to become a champion! Welcome to the Academy."

Four days later Danny received a letter in the post from the Teddy Tennis Academy. It read:

Dear Danny,

Firstly, well done on becoming a member of the Teddy Tennis Academy. I am looking forward to teaching you as a stage three Cub Cadet.

Teddy Tennis training starts on Saturday 6th May at 8.30 in the morning. Please come along to Court One in your new Teddy Tennis outfit.

Good luck and see you then.

HEAD TED
Teddy Tennis Academy

Chapter Four

Danny's first day

(Saturday 6th May)

Danny had a very restless night. He was thinking about all the things that could go wrong on the important day. He had even written a list of things he should and shouldn't do:

Must tie my own shoelaces

Must take my Teddy Tennis racket

Must remember my packed lunch and drinks

Must stay calm

…and last but not least,

Must not fidget with my ears when listening to Head Ted.

1. must tie my own
   shoelaces
2. must take my
   teddy tennis racket
3. must remember my
   Packed lunch and drinks
4. must stay calm
5. must not fidget with
   my ears whenlistening
   to Hed Ted

Danny Bear

Danny arrived at the Academy with Johnny Mac and Chloë. Head Ted was there to greet him and lifted his paw for silence. A hush came over the Academy. "Cub Cadets of the Teddy Tennis Academy," Head Ted began, "This is a special day. Today we welcome Danny Bear, younger brother of Johnny Mac and Chloë, to the Academy as a stage three Cub Cadet. Let us put our paws together and wish him the best of luck."

Cheers and clapping echoed around the Academy.

"This is the beginning of something big," thought Danny.

Head Ted gathered all the stage three Cub Cadets together and sat them down on the grass. He had been a famous Teddy Tennis champion when he was younger.

"Listen, you lucky cubs. You are going to learn the secrets of becoming great Teddy Tennis players. You'll learn to be really good at running, hopping, skipping, jumping and all sorts of ball skills. These are the 'Bear Essentials.' What are they Cub Cadets?" shouted Head Ted.

"Bear Essentials!" shouted back Danny and the other Cub Cadets.

"Once you can do all these things, you will learn how to use your Teddy Tennis racket, and how to hit Teddy Tennis balls so they can fly over the net and bounce into the court. So before we start, are there any questions?" said Head Ted, looking around.

"Yes," said Danny. "Why has my Teddy Tennis t-shirt got a large red paw mark on the sleeve?"

"Can any Cub Cadets answer Danny's question?"

"Yes, I can," said Amanda Panda. "There are three Cub Cadet stages. Each stage has a different colour. We are the Red Paw Stage Cub Cadets and we have a red paw on our t-shirts. This means we are beginners. The next level is orange. The top stage is green. Red, orange, green: just like the colours of traffic lights."

"Well done, Amanda!" said Head Ted.

He then walked over to his sports bag, pulled out a chunky yellow CD player and put in a CD that said; 'Teddy Tennis Red Paw Rhythms.'

Head Ted spoke again, "Cub Cadets, one of my secrets in learning to play Teddy Tennis is music! Music helps us move around the court more easily. It helps us to swing the racket at the ball so we can hit it, just right. Copy me while we warm up to the Teddy Tennis Song, Hip Hop Tidley Bop."

He pressed the 'play' button and started to jog around the court in time to the music. "Follow me!" he shouted.

All the Cub Cadets jumped up and followed Head Ted. Danny found himself jogging, jumping and hopping around the court, copying all the movements that Head Ted and the other Cub cadets made.

Eventually the music stopped. "Every bear ready for our first game?" Head Ted panted.

"Yes!" cried all the Cub Cadets, jumping up and down.

"It's called 'Throw, Bounce and Catch.' Find yourselves a partner."

Danny found himself face to face with a big ginger cub with a baseball cap.
"I am Boris. Do as I do and you will be okay."

"Strange voice," thought Danny, "must come from somewhere that isn't here."

"Each Cub Cadet must pick up a Teddy Tennis ball and then
throw, bounce and catch it. Just follow the words to the song,"
said Head Ted.

The song started and the fun began.

Danny had done a little bit of catching before
in his training so he was looking forward to this.
Boris threw the ball so that it bounced and then
Danny tried to catch it. Then Danny threw the
ball back to Boris, bouncing it on the ground
in the same way. It was great fun.

The Cub Cadets played many other games
including 'Over My Shoulder,' which helped
Danny with his first Teddy Tennis stroke,
the forehand. As the day went on, Danny began
to realise that Teddy Tennis was tougher than
he thought but he loved every minute of it.